TONY JEFFERSON IN

Double Back

Agnes M. Hagen

D1280924

New Readers Press

For Christina, who gave me a chance.

Double Back
ISBN 1-56420-276-3
Copyright © 2001
New Readers Press
U.S. Publishing Division of Laubach Literacy
1320 Jamesville Avenue, Syracuse, New York 13210

Printed in the United States of America
9 8 7 6 5 4 3 2 1

Director of Acquisitions and Development: Christina Jagger
Content Editor: Terrie Lipke
Copy Editor: Judi Lauber
Production Director: Heather Witt
Designer: Kimbrly Koennecke
Cover Designer: Kimbrly Koennecke
Cover Illustrator: James P. Wallace
Production Specialist: Alexander Jones

All proceeds from the sale of New Readers Press materials support literacy programs in the United States and worldwide.

Chapter 1

The suspect knew we had him surrounded. His face was filled with anger and fear. With nothing left to lose, he raised his gun and pulled the trigger. I saw my partner go down. A flurry of shots followed, then silence.

My partner was more than just a co-worker; he was like family. And now the man I'd worked side by side with for 10 years was dying in a Baltimore alley.

He was a cop who loved his wife

and kids. He coached Little League on his days off. Now he was gone because a frantic criminal did not want to die alone.

My name is Tony Jefferson. I grew up here in Baltimore, Maryland. My whole life I wanted to be a cop. Now, for the first time, I'm not sure what I want to do.

In school I was a patrol boy. I helped other kids cross the street safely. I patrolled the school grounds like I was walking a beat. Police work is in my blood.

Now I'm 31 years old, and I still can't imagine being anything else. But the thought of starting over with a new partner was more than I could take. I quit the force right after the funeral.

My parents came for a visit to try to cheer me up. But Baltimore just wasn't the same for me anymore. Everywhere I looked I saw cops and criminals. My mother suggested a change of scenery.

So when my grandmother called to invite me down to Virginia, I jumped at the chance. Maybe visiting my grandparents in rural Bath County would be just what I needed.

There are few folks in this world as welcoming as Mamaw and Papaw. Honest, that's what I call them to this day.

So this morning, I gassed up the Chevy and threw my battered suitcase in the trunk. I told my German shepherd, Chance, that we were going for a ride, and he eagerly jumped in the car beside me. And we headed south. After I passed the traffic around Washington, D.C., there were fewer and fewer cars. It was a sunny day, and the closer I got to the mountains, the more beautiful they were. Just getting away from the city made me feel calmer already.

Nearing my grandparents' home, I stopped at a little store in Buffalo Gap to pick up some of Papaw's favorite pipe tobacco and a box of chocolates for Mamaw. The same old guy I remembered from years ago was still running the store. He saw me and smiled. "I know who's going to be happy to see you," he said. "How's life in the big city?"

"You don't know what you've been missing," I said sadly. He looked puzzled. I think he sensed that I didn't drive 200 miles just for a friendly visit.

"Well, lad," he added, "this is a peaceful place. I don't know what your trouble is, but being here will help you get over it. Now why don't you get yourself a fishing pole and go down to the lake?"

"That's not a bad idea," I replied, thinking it over. "I might just do that."

He was a good salesman. I left the store with a brand-new fishing rod, a tackle box, and plenty of bait. I hadn't fished in years, but suddenly it seemed like the best idea I'd ever heard.

Chapter 2

As I drove up to my grandparents' house, I noticed how little the place had changed. It had been a dozen years since my last visit, but everything was just as I remembered. Chance was whimpering with excitement. I opened the car door, and he leaped out to greet the dogs, cats, and goats that now surrounded us. Mamaw opened the door of the house, wiping her hands on her apron.

"Tony!" she cried. "How's my

wonderful grandson?" I bounded up the porch steps and gave the white-haired woman a bear hug.

"You look great!" I said. "Where's Papaw?"

"He's been fishing since dawn," she grinned. "You know that man could never stay still for a minute. And he always says that fall is the best time for fishin'. Come on in, Tony. I've fried up some chicken for lunch."

I didn't know I was hungry till I smelled the fried chicken and spoon bread. Mamaw pressed a cup of spiced hot apple cider into my hand and settled me in front of a plate of food.

"You know I've missed you, Tony," she said. "But there's another reason I'm glad you're here. Since you're a police detective, I was hoping you could help our neighbors, the Simons.

"Mrs. Simon is a widow, and her 25-year-old daughter is missing. It's only been a day, but she's worried. It's just not like Dawn to take off without letting someone know where she is going. The local police don't seem to be helping. Mrs. Simon and her daughter, Julie, are frantic. I've told them about you, Tony. Do you think you could help them?"

I felt a knot in my stomach. "Mamaw, I might as well tell you now, I left the force. After watching my partner get killed, I couldn't deal with it anymore. That's why I'm here. I have to think about my life and decide what to do now."

"I know, Tony, your mother called and told me all that," Mamaw replied. "But you know you're good at this sort of thing. And besides, you don't have to be a cop to find a missing girl. Anyway, Mrs. Simon and Julie are coming to supper tonight. Just talk to them and see if there's anything you can do. OK?"

I gulped. "They just *happen* to be

coming to supper tonight?" I asked. "I've been set up!"

"Eat, Tony. Your spoon bread is getting cold," smiled Mamaw. "If you hurry, you can spend some time down at the lake with Papaw. He'll be real glad to see you."

I still felt uneasy, but I'm a sucker for a home-cooked meal. I began shoveling the spoon bread and chicken into my mouth. The taste was heavenly. I'd forgotten how delicious Mamaw's cooking was.

***

After an hour fishing with Papaw, I was ready for a nap. I couldn't believe how relaxed I felt. I dozed off in a rocker on the front porch. I woke to the aroma of dinner coming from the kitchen.

When I walked into the dining room, Mrs. Simon was just sitting down. She was a tall woman who wore her graying hair pulled back in a tight bun. Her eyes, behind thick glasses, were sad. Tears welled up as she spoke of her missing daughter.

"It's not like Dawn to disappear without a word," said Mrs. Simon. "She always tells us where she's going. And she didn't show up for work today either."

"Even her boyfriend, Sam, doesn't know where she is," added Julie. "I just know something's wrong."

Julie Simon was probably in her early 20s, but she was unlike any of the women I'd known back in Baltimore. She wore no makeup, yet she had a fresh, natural beauty.

Honesty and intelligence shone from her vivid blue eyes. Her skin glowed with good health, but her hands showed the calluses of hard work. I wanted to know more about this woman. Maybe helping the Simon family would be interesting, after all.

At any rate, I found myself saying,

"Mrs. Simon, Julie, I'd like to help you find Dawn. I won't make any promises, but I'll do what I can."

"You see," Mamaw cried. "I told you Tony would help. He's my favorite grandson!"

"Mamaw, I'm your only grandson," I replied.

"A minor detail, my boy, a minor detail," chuckled Papaw.

Chapter 3

I walked Julie home and asked if I could meet with her the next day. I hoped she could tell me more about Dawn. She smiled and asked, "Do you like dogs?"

"I sure do," I answered. "My dog, Chance, is here with me."

"Good!" Julie said. "I promised weeks ago that I would be a judge at our annual dog show tomorrow. Why don't you and Chance come? Maybe Chance can enter one of the contests.

It's just a local show for animal lovers, so you're welcome to join in. And we can talk more about Dawn."

"That sounds like fun," I said. "Chance was trained to trail and catch criminals. He can follow a week-old trail like it was just made an hour ago. But he was injured in the line of duty, so now he's just a civilian, like me."

Julie grinned. "I'll come pick you up at seven A.M.," she said.

I didn't have any trouble waking early. I smelled coffee brewing and bacon frying. I looked out the window at another lovely fall day. I wondered what it would be like to live in a place like this year in and year out. Would I miss the fast pace of a big city? I pushed that thought aside and went to the breakfast table.

I had just finished my bacon, eggs, and biscuits when a truck beeped outside. Chance and I piled into the pickup with Julie and headed off to

Stanton. We made small talk, and then the topic turned to Julie's sister, Dawn.

"We still haven't heard from Dawn. The local police say they've looked everywhere, Tony. They've questioned Mom and me and Dawn's friends. I think they should have spent more time questioning her ex-boyfriend, Rick. When Dawn dumped him, he didn't take it well at all. He says that he hasn't talked to Dawn in months. But I still don't trust him," Julie said.

"Did the police search your home?" I asked.

"Yes," Julie answered. "But, Tony, I went to school with Jed, the deputy who's investigating. He has all the goodwill in the world, but he's never worked on a case this serious before. In a big city like Baltimore, you probably had missing people to search for all the time. You must know a lot more about this than he does. Why don't you talk to Jed and see if he could use your help?"

"For one thing, I'm afraid that he'd think I was trying to take over," I said. "For another thing, I came down here to get away from police work, Julie. I'll be honest with you, I'm not sure this is what I want to do right now."

Julie looked disappointed, but she wasn't giving up. "Tony, for what it's worth, I believe in you already," Julie smiled. "I was sorry to hear about your partner. I know what it's like to lose someone close to you. My father died last year. Maybe helping us will take your mind off the pain. It's a lot to ask of someone I just met yesterday. But I sense that you are a strong person. Maybe finding my sister will prove your career isn't over."

Julie felt guilty about keeping her promise to work at the dog show. I told her that we should try to enjoy ourselves as long as we were there. Later there would be plenty of time to talk about Dawn. I tried to reassure her that Dawn would probably call or return on her own.

We pulled into a park in the center of town, and dozens of barking dogs drowned out any further conversation. The contests were lots of fun. A poodle dressed like a cowboy won for the best costume. And a hound dog was judged to look most like his owner. A tiny Chihuahua won a huge blue ribbon for having the prettiest eyes.

Chance, however, stole the show. I asked a young boy if he would hide and let Chance try to find him. The boy eagerly handed me one of his shoes, and I covered Chance's eyes with a blindfold. The boy then ran and hid under the gazebo, flattening himself amidst dead leaves. Chance sniffed at the shoe and took off. In less than a minute he was barking happily as he tugged on the boy's other shoe. Everyone clapped as Julie pinned a blue ribbon to Chance's collar.

Riding back in the truck, I turned to Julie. "I've been thinking about what you said earlier," I said. "You have good instincts about people, Julie. I think it will do me good to try to be useful."

Julie grinned. "Mom always says Dawn got the good looks and I got the common sense," she said.

When she dropped Chance and me off at my grandparents' home, Julie handed me a picture of her sister. "This is my favorite photo of Dawn," she said softly. "If we still haven't heard from her by morning, you will go look for her, won't you, Tony?"

Chapter 4

The next morning I found the tiny police station behind the post office. Crime fighting was not big business in Bath County. The deputy was a tall fellow in a sharp blue uniform. Behind him on a bulletin board I spotted a copy of the photo that Julie had given me.

"Hi," I said, offering my hand. "I'm Tony Jefferson, Catherine and Al Jefferson's grandson."

That brought a smile to the deputy's face. "The Jeffersons are great folks," he said. "My dad goes deer hunting with Al. And everyone in Bath County knows Catherine—for her cooking *and* her kindness. Want some coffee?" I nodded and sat across from him. "My name's Hawkins, Jed Hawkins."

For a few minutes we sipped coffee and swapped police stories. Then talk turned to Dawn Simon. "We don't get many cases like this," Jed admitted. "For the most part we deal with traffic accidents, hunting violations, and family fights. Sometimes kids run away from home."

"This case is different," I said. "According to her mother and sister, Dawn wasn't restless or unhappy. And they said she didn't pack anything before she left." The deputy nodded. "Look," I said, leaning back in my chair. "I was a detective on the force in Baltimore. I don't want to take over your job. But I do have experience in handling cases like this. I'm willing to help if I can."

Jed smiled. "I don't mind if you ask around some," he replied. "You say that you're friendly with the Simon family, take a look around their house. Maybe I missed something. Just let me know what you find, if you find anything."

"Fair enough," I replied. "I'm not here to show off. I'm just doing a favor for Mamaw," I said, with a chuckle. Truth was, I was beginning to look forward to this.

Jed shook my hand warmly. "You could talk to Dawn's boyfriend, Sam Otis. He's a country music singer, lives up on Pig Run. He might know more than he's letting on."

Later that afternoon, I forced my wheezing Chevy up Bath County's hills to Pig Run. I only had to stop once for directions. From there, I just followed the music to Sam's cabin. Three young men sat on the porch with banjos and guitars.

I walked slowly up to the cabin humming along with the familiar bluegrass melody. "Hello there, stranger," called one fellow in an old straw hat. "Can I help you?" he asked.

"I hope so," I replied. "I'm Tony Jefferson. I'm helping Deputy Hawkins with the search for Dawn Simon." The young man rose to his feet and stuck out his hand.

"The name's Sam Otis, and I'm looking for Dawn Simon too. Come on up here and have a seat." The other two musicians went inside. I took a seat on the porch, next to Sam. "I've heard that you're a cop, Tony. Folks around here are talking about you. Everybody knows everything in a small town like this.

"I've been worried sick about Dawn. She's been gone for two days now, without even a phone call. That's not like Dawn. Last year she went to Nashville. She wasn't there ten minutes when she phoned me. We're pretty tight. In fact, I've been thinking of asking her to marry me now that my group is making some real money."

"Does Dawn have any enemies?" I asked.

"I don't know anyone who doesn't like her," he replied. "With that computer of hers she's made friends all over the world. Her ex-boyfriend, Rick, says he hates her, but I think he's still in love with her. The cops say he wasn't around when Dawn disappeared. Though it wouldn't surprise me if he was involved. Rick hates everybody, me most of all. I bet he'd do anything to get Dawn back."

Sam seemed like an honest, straightforward sort of fellow. I believed that he really loved Dawn.

Chapter 5

Early the following morning, I ran into Deputy Hawkins in town. I asked if he'd found anything new.

"A patrolman from the next county found Dawn's car," Jed said. "They got ahold of me this morning. It looks like there's a problem with the fuel line. I'm having it towed to the police station."

"Where was it?" I asked. "Did you find anything else?"

"Her car was on the side of the road, between here and Rockfish," Jed said.

"There was no sign of Dawn."

"Let me know when her car gets here," I said. "I'd like to take a look at it. In the meantime, I'm going to call Mrs. Simon and see if I can go over there."

Jed went on his way. He seemed worried. I called Mrs. Simon to ask if I could come over, and she invited me to lunch. Chance was invited, too.

Papaw had given Mrs. Simon a hefty trout from his latest fishing trip. She had panfried it in butter. There was also fresh corn from a farm nearby. And for dessert, Julie had picked tart apples and baked them into a pie.

"I could easily get used to eating like this!" I said. "People around here really work hard for their food."

"We worked even harder before my Tom died," Mrs. Simon said sadly. "It's been almost a year since the accident. The tractor hit a rut and flipped over on him. We don't plant much anymore."

"Now enough of that, Mom," Julie said, quickly changing the subject. "Tony is here to look around in Dawn's room. Maybe he'll find a clue to where she's gone.

"It's been three days now. We haven't touched this room. We didn't want to disturb anything," Julie said as we climbed the stairs. "You never know, Tony. Sometimes what you're looking for is right in front of you, but you just don't see it."

I nodded. "Do you mind if I call Chance in? It might be helpful if he picked up Dawn's scent."

"Please do," Julie smiled. "If what I saw at the dog show is any indication, he's got a terrific nose." I whistled, and the large dog bounded up the stairs behind us.

Dawn's room was quite tidy. Her bedspread didn't have a wrinkle in it. Dresses and slacks hung neatly in her closet. Her shoes were lined up on the floor. Chance stuck his nose under the bed. Nothing seemed out of place. A fancy porcelain statue adorned the top of the dresser. Julie said it was a gift from Sam Otis.

Photos of family and friends were stuck around the mirror frame. As Julie identified these people, I wrote down their names. The graceful hand of the porcelain lady seemed to point to a faded photo of a baby girl dressed in pink.

"Cute kid," I remarked. "Who is it?"

"That's the picture of Dawn that the social worker gave Mom and Dad," Julie said simply. "Mom never talks about Dawn's adoption. She always wanted Dawn to feel that she was just as much her daughter as I am."

"I had no idea that Dawn was adopted," I said. "Mamaw never mentioned it."

"I guess we didn't think it was

important," Julie replied.

Removing the picture from the mirror, I looked at it very carefully. The side that was stuck in the mirror frame appeared to be trimmed off. "Julie," I asked, "do you have a magnifying glass?"

"Sure," she replied. "I'll get it. Mom uses one for her needlework." In a minute she was back.

"Now," I said softly. "Take a look at the edge of this photo. See where the dress is cut off? Do you see something else?" We sat on Dawn's bed and examined the photo.

"It looks like part of a tiny arm. Do you think there was another baby in the picture?" Julie asked. "Maybe the social worker took a photo of two babies together."

"Maybe," I answered. But I wondered, silently, about the connection between Dawn and the other baby.

Double Back

Suddenly Julie jumped up. "Dawn had really gotten interested in looking for her birth mother lately. She didn't want Mom to know because she was afraid of hurting her feelings. Do you think that Dawn's disappearance could have something to do with her search for her birth family?"

Chapter 6

Maybe we were finally onto something. "Tell me about Dawn's search for her birth mother," I told Julie.

"Dawn used her computer to go to web sites where adoptees could look for messages from their birth parents," Julie replied. She opened a laptop computer on Dawn's desk. "And she had posted messages on Internet bulletin boards looking for information."

"Julie, could I take the computer home?" I asked. "I'd like to check out some of these sites. Maybe I can find out how much she knew."

"I'd be glad to help you," Julie answered. "We'd better have something to tell Mom, though. If she comes in here, she'll notice the laptop is missing."

"Why not tell her the truth, Julie," I suggested. "It's going to come out in the end. Besides, maybe your mother knows something that will help us."

Mrs. Simon quickly agreed to tell me anything if I thought it might help me find Dawn. Over iced tea, she told a sad story. Early in her marriage, Mrs. Simon gave birth to a premature infant that lived only a few hours. The doctor was not sure she would be able to carry another child. Julie listened quietly, shocked by her mother's openness.

"My husband and I were terribly

unhappy," Mrs. Simon said. "So when this lawyer told us that he knew of a baby up for adoption, we rushed to his office. We didn't care to know about Dawn's birth parents. She would be our child, that was all that mattered."

I showed Mrs. Simon the photo. "Do you know where the rest of this photo is?" I asked. "It looks like there was another baby beside Dawn when the photo was taken."

"That's all the lawyer gave us. I don't know anything about another baby," she replied. "I was so happy about getting Dawn that I didn't ask many questions."

I wrote down the name of the lawyer, and Julie walked me to my car. "Do you have something that Dawn has worn recently?" I asked her. "I'd like Chance to have something with Dawn's scent."

"Sure," Julie said. She ran into the house and came back out with a blue sweatshirt. "Dawn wears this old thing all the time."

When I got home I searched the phone book for the lawyer who had handled Dawn's adoption. After several phone calls, I learned that the man died more than 15 years ago. No one knew where his files might be, if they existed at all.

I hooked up Dawn's computer when I got home. By the time I started looking through her files, it was dinnertime. Then Jed Hawkins called. "I just thought you'd want to know I picked up Dawn's ex-boyfriend, Rick, this afternoon," he said. "He was driving too fast, with an open six-pack of beer in the car. He kept mumbling, but he wasn't making much sense. If you want to talk to him, he's in the holding cell for now."

I thanked Jed and told him I'd be there shortly. After I finished eating, I headed for the station. I could hear

Rick's snores before I opened the door. "He looks peaceful now, but he was a handful when I picked him up," said Jed. "That guy is one mean drunk!"

Jed hollered to Rick to wake him up. He was far from sober, and refused to talk about Dawn or Sam. "You're not going to pin that on me!" Rick shouted. "I was at army camp all weekend. There are at least fifty men who will back me up, too. Sam Otis probably has her stashed away someplace," Rick mumbled.

"Maybe they even eloped. Who knows what he would do," Rick said. "Sam stole her from me—so what's to stop him from taking her from her family?" With that, Rick rolled over on his bunk and fell back to sleep.

Before I left, I asked Jed where Rick's car was. "Out back, in our lot," Jed said. "And Dawn's car is back there now, too. I'll show you."

On a hunch, I took Chance with me

Double Back

to see if he could pick up Dawn's scent. Except for locating an empty liquor bottle under the seat, Chance didn't seem interested in Rick's car at all.

Then I opened the door to Dawn's small car. Chance recognized her scent right away and excitedly sniffed every inch of the car. A folder on the backseat contained some computer printouts. I noticed that there were printouts from some adoption sites.

"Do you mind if I take these papers with me, Jed?" I asked. "Julie and I are checking out Dawn's computer to see if we can find any clues. These addresses might help."

"No problem, Tony," he answered. "We all want to find Dawn."

Dawn's car was as neat as her room. So it seemed odd when Chance found a candy bag on the floor. There were just two wrapped candies left inside. She must have been snacking during her drive.

Chapter 7

I returned home to find Julie hard at work on the computer. "I couldn't wait to get started," she explained. "So your grandmother let me in. I already found a list of sites Dawn visited," she announced excitedly.

"I'm impressed," I answered. And I really was. "I found these Internet addresses in her car, but it looks like you beat me to it."

"Look," Julie said pointing at the

screen. "You just go to the activity file and look up its history. Here are the sites Dawn has visited recently. I've been checking into them, one by one." She handled the keyboard and mouse like a pro. I think I remember Mamaw saying that she had an administrative job. She must use a computer at work.

Then we both saw it! A notice was posted on the message board within a site Julie was checking.

Birth mother in search

of daughter born March 7,

25 years ago, Rockfish, VA.

"That's Dawn's birth date!" Julie exclaimed.

Someone was looking for a baby girl born in Rockfish on the same day as Dawn. "Let's reply right away," I said. "We need to know if Dawn contacted this person."

"Rockfish is only about seventy miles from here," Julie said. "Maybe the person who placed the ad will send us her address. I've tried to get into Dawn's e-mail account, but I don't have her password."

Just as we were sending our reply to the message, Mamaw appeared in the doorway. "You're not going to believe this, but now Sam Otis has disappeared. A friend of his just called to see if he was here. No one has seen him all day. His band was supposed to play at the tavern this evening, but Sam never showed up."

"Has anyone seen his car?" I asked.

"Not that I know of," said Mamaw. "He didn't tell the rest of the band that he was going anywhere. He seems to have vanished, just like Dawn."

"Did anyone call the police?" Julie asked.

"Not yet," Mamaw replied.

It was late, but Julie and I drove over to the police station. My mind was racing now that a second person was missing. Were the disappearances related?

Jed Hawkins peered up from behind a pile of paperwork on his cluttered desk. "It's kind of late for a friendly visit. You two must be here for a reason," he said.

"That's right," I answered as Julie and I sat down. "Have you heard that Sam Otis is missing?"

"Hmm, that's interesting," said Jed, tapping his pen on the desk. "I always thought he knew more than he was telling. He's involved in Dawn's disappearance somehow. I can feel it."

"Speaking of Dawn, we found some information on her computer," said Julie. "I really think we're onto something, don't you, Tony?" I nodded and handed Jed a printout of the bulletin board message.

"This doesn't give us much to go on," Jed said thoughtfully. "But maybe

Dawn decided to play detective and track down the woman who placed this message on the Web. Rockfish is a small town in the next county. I know the sheriff over there. I could call tomorrow and talk to him."

On the way home, Julie turned to me. "Jed's right. Rockfish *is* small," she said, "just like Stanton. I'll bet everybody knows everybody else's business. Why don't we drive over there in the morning? We can ask a few questions ourselves."

"Now you're beginning to talk like a cop," I chuckled.

Chapter 8

Rockfish was a quiet village nestled high in the Blue Ridge Mountains. Despite the scenic beauty of the area, it was clearly not a wealthy community. Many homes were small and in disrepair. A huge old factory building sat empty and deserted, like a ghost town.

Julie and I stopped first at a drugstore on Main Street. It seemed to be a hub of activity. There, we bought snacks and chatted with a middle-aged woman behind the counter. We asked her some general questions about the town and its people. Then I asked if she knew anyone who had given up a baby for adoption 25 years ago.

"People around here don't have a lot of money since the shoe factory shut down," she responded. "That was about twenty-five years ago. Lots of folks left town to find work. Those who stayed might not have been able to afford another mouth to feed," she said matter-of-factly.

"Do you know of anyone who might have recently been looking for a long-lost adopted daughter?" I asked, just hoping for a break.

"Well, Mrs. Thurman did finally get rid of that nasty old husband of hers a few months back," she said. "I've heard that he forced her to give up a baby. The rumor is that she gave up the twin sister of that girl of hers, Eve. I'd say Eve is about twenty-five."

"Do you know where I can find Mrs. Thurman?" I asked, trying to contain my excitement.

"Just don't you go upsetting that poor soul! She's had a hard life. From what I hear, that husband of hers put her through hell. She's just now getting her life back."

The woman reluctantly gave me directions to Mrs. Thurman's house. The Thurmans had moved to nearby Cooper Springs after the shoe factory closed. It took about 40 minutes to get there. Chance was enjoying all the riding around.

Julie and I trudged up a narrow path to the front door. Rebecca Thurman's home was an ancient blue trailer spotted with rust. A cheery patch of bright yellow flowers greeted me near the door. The woman who answered my knock looked as if life had beaten her to the ground. The sadness etched on her face made her look older than her years.

"Mrs. Thurman?" I asked. "My name is Tony Jefferson. I'm looking for someone you might know. Her name is Dawn Simon and she was born on March seventh, twenty-five years ago." At that Rebecca Thurman quietly began to sob.

"All these years!" she cried. "After all these years Dawn said she was coming to meet me, but she never arrived. I was beginning to think it was just a cruel joke."

"Dawn disappeared a few days ago. I'm trying to find out where she is," I replied gently. "May I come in?"

"Of course," she answered, opening the door wider.

The inside of the trailer was well kept. The furniture was old and faded, but everything looked spotlessly clean. "You put a message on a computer bulletin board recently," I began.

Double Back

"Yes," she said. "A friend of mine has a computer. After my husband took off, she said she'd help me try to find my baby. While he was around, he'd hit me if he even heard me talk about Dawn. My husband wasn't all bad, Mr. Jefferson, but when I had the twins we were just sixteen. He didn't even have a job. He told me that he couldn't afford two babies and a wife. He wanted me to give both of my little girls up for adoption. My parents agreed with him. I'd named them Dawn and Eve. They were so beautiful, so perfect."

She broke down again. "There isn't a day I don't think of Dawn. When someone answered my message, I still couldn't believe it was really my daughter. I could hardly wait to meet her and see, but she never came. I figured it was too good to be true."

"How did you manage to keep Eve?" I asked.

"Dawn was a little bigger and stronger, so she was adopted right away. Then I became so depressed after they took her from me that I threatened to kill myself," Rebecca sobbed. "Finally, when my parents agreed to give us a little money, my husband said I could keep Eve. But I never stopped missing my Dawn."

"Where's Eve now?" I asked. "Does she know she has a sister?"

"Eve works at the diner in town," Rebecca replied. "She'll be there till after supper. I haven't even told her that she has a sister. I didn't want to get her hopes up and have her be disappointed, like I am."

Chapter 9

On our way out, we promised to let Mrs. Thurman know as soon as we found Dawn. "Let's go and see Eve," Julie said. "Even if she doesn't know anything about all this, I'd still like to meet her."

"OK," I said, "but we should be careful what we say. Her mother should be the one to tell her about Dawn."

We drove back toward the main street in Cooper Springs. As we entered the dimly lit diner, Julie gasped and grabbed my arm. Eve Thurman was standing near the counter. She looked just like Julie's sister, Dawn. Even their hairstyles were similar. "Dawn?" Julie asked, in shock.

"You're the second person to call me that today," Eve answered. "Why, that young man in the booth over there just told me the strangest story. He says I am the spitting image of his girlfriend, Dawn."

Sam Otis was sitting in a booth, drinking coffee. He looked up and motioned for us to join him.

"What are you doing here?" I asked. "Everyone's looking for you!"

"Well, I got to thinking after our little talk," Sam said. "And I wondered if there wasn't some clue to Dawn's whereabouts in her e-mail. She's always on that darn computer lately. I've watched her access her mail so many times that I was sure I could get into her account.

"So I went to the library to use the computer. It took hours for me to hit on the right password and get into Dawn's e-mail account. Luckily I'm a friend of the librarian, and she let me stay and work after closing. I knew Dawn had been scouring those adoption bulletin boards. So I thought maybe she had made contact with someone. Finally I got in. There was a message from a Mrs. Thurman. It gave her address here, in Cooper Springs. But it didn't look like Dawn had read the message.

"Then I must have dozed off. I woke up when the library opened and headed straight here. I just stopped for a cup of coffee before going to Mrs. Thurman's, and I ran into Eve."

"We looked into Dawn's computer activity too," Julie said. "Dawn saw a message that Mrs. Thurman posted looking for a baby girl born in Rockfish twenty-five years ago. Dawn must not have waited for a response. I'll bet she headed straight for Rockfish."

"That would explain where her car was found," I said.

"But where is Dawn?" asked Sam.

I told him that we had just come from Rebecca Thurman's. "She got Dawn's message saying she was coming, but Dawn never showed up."

"So this is really true?" Eve asked, stepping over to the booth. "I do have a twin sister?"

"Yes," replied Julie, "my adopted sister, Dawn, is really your twin."

"Oh, I just can't believe all of this!" said Eve. "I need to talk to my mother. Why didn't she tell me?"

"Your mother didn't want to tell you until she was sure she'd found Dawn," I explained. "And since Dawn didn't arrive when she said she would, your mother was afraid that she'd never find her."

Double Back

"I'm going to get someone to cover for me and go straight home," Eve said. "I think my Mom and I have a lot to talk about. Please call us right away when you find my sister!"

I told her that with the three of us and Chance hot on the trail, we'd surely find Dawn soon. Sam left a generous tip and we headed out.

"Since there are three of us, let's split up," I suggested. "You two can go to Rockfish in Sam's car. Walk around town and ask if anyone has seen or heard from Dawn. I'll drive to where Dawn's car was found and see if the police overlooked any clues. Then I'll make my way toward Rockfish and meet you both there."

Chapter 10

I took Chance and drove to where Jed said he'd found Dawn's car. Some burnt-out police flares marked the spot. Dawn's sweatshirt was still in my car. I let Chance take a good sniff. Then I opened the door.

Chance nosed around where Dawn's car was and then just kept walking. He seemed to pick up a trail straight down the side of the road, heading toward Rockfish. I held Chance's leash tight so he wouldn't get away from me. There were wooded hills in every direction. I hoped Dawn wasn't lost out there somewhere.

We must have walked more than a mile, at Chance's steady gait. Then he lost the scent. There were tire marks on the side of the road, like someone had pulled over. Chance sniffed toward the woods, and even across the road, but didn't pick up anything. Maybe someone pulled over and gave Dawn a ride. Since the tracks were on the same side of the road as Dawn's car, my guess is that the person who picked her up was headed for Rockfish, too.

I wanted to be sure that the trail had ended. Maybe the tracks had nothing to do with Dawn. So Chance and I kept walking. He sniffed along the shoulder of the road, and sometimes he sniffed at the edge of the woods.

Soon Chance picked up another trail. An old, overgrown dirt road meandered uphill. Chance followed the dirt road, slowly at first. When he started walking faster, I knew he was onto something.

Chance stopped suddenly and barked. On the ground near his paw was a candy wrapper. It was the same kind of candy that was in Dawn's car. Chance was very excited.

He tugged at the leash for me to let him continue on. We seemed to be following a seldom-used trail. The ground was soft and covered with leaves and pine needles. I saw a few footprints and some fairly fresh tire tracks.

Along the way, Chance occasionally found another candy wrapper. Maybe Dawn was leaving a trail so she could find her way back to the road again. Or maybe she was hoping to catch someone's attention.

The woods became even more dense as we went along. Without Chance, I would be lost. Chance and I were both panting, as the hill got steeper. Then up ahead, I saw something in the trees. It was a small cabin. Chance led me right to the door.

Chance started barking. He jumped at the door, and it fell open. The old cabin had only two rooms, so I could see right away that it was empty. But on an old wooden table there was another candy wrapper.

"Well, Chance, now what do we do?" I asked. Chance responded by barking loudly. It echoed in the woods. Then I thought I heard a voice, far off. Chance barked again. And again, I heard the voice.

"Help!" the voice cried, weakly. This time, Chance turned and ran behind the cabin and into the trees.

"Help me!" The voice grew louder. It sounded like a woman's voice.

"We're coming!" I hollered back. Chance came to a sudden stop at the edge of a steep bank. When I looked down, I could see a woman sitting near the edge of a stream.

"Are you Dawn Simon?" I asked.

"Yes. Who are you?" she asked.

"I'm Tony Jefferson. Your mother asked me to help find you," I said.

"I'm glad she did! I fell down the bank and twisted my ankle," Dawn said. "I don't think I can climb back up. Can you help me?"

I looked around. "I'll be right back," I said. "Chance, stay here." I ran back to the cabin where I found a hunk of old rope. Then I returned to the stream.

"If I lower this rope for you to hang onto, do you think you can climb up?" I asked.

"I'll try," Dawn said. "There's no sense in you getting stuck down here too!"

I tied one end of the rope to a tree and dropped the other end down to Dawn. She was a little wobbly on her feet. But she grabbed the rope strongly.

Double Back

"OK, now," I said. "I'm going to pull up slowly while you climb the bank. Let me know if you feel you might fall."

Dawn pushed with her good leg and held the rope tightly. Slowly, she came closer to the top of the bank. Finally I could reach down and grab one of her arms and help pull her up the rest of the way.

"Are you OK?" I asked Dawn.

"I think so. My ankle's sore, but it's not broken. And I'm just tired and hungry. I've had nothing but candy to eat for days."

"I'm glad you had that candy," I said. "Without it, Chance and I might have lost your trail."

"I was hoping to follow that trail back to the road. But by the time I got out of the cabin, I was so thirsty; I didn't think I'd make it. An old map in the cabin showed where the stream was. But I was so anxious to find water, I guess I wasn't really watching where I was walking, and I fell down the bank. Soon afterward I heard a dog barking, and I knew someone was nearby."

"It's a long way back to my car," I told Dawn. "Can you make it?"

"Oh, yes," she replied. "The thought of getting out of here is enough to keep me going! But I might have to lean on you a little."

"That's fine," I said. "I just want to get you home to your family." When I said the word *family*, I realized that Dawn had not yet met her other family. We'd have a lot to talk about on the way down this hill.

Chapter 11

"How did you end up in the woods, Dawn?" I asked. "The police found your car quite far from here."

"Yes, I know," she replied. "It stalled on my way to Rockfish. I couldn't get it started again."

"You were going to Rockfish to meet your birth mother," I said.

"How did you know?" she asked. "I didn't tell anyone."

"Well, actually, I'm a police detective from Baltimore," I said. "I came here to see my grandparents—Catherine and Al Jefferson. Your mother and sister asked me to help find you. Julie found the web site message about a baby born in Rockfish on your birth date. We had a feeling that's where you went."

"Oh, no," she said. "That poor woman was expecting me days ago."

"Yes, Mrs. Thurman," I added. "I've met her. She knows we're looking for you. Sam and Julie are in Rockfish. But you should have waited for Mrs. Thurman's response to your e-mail. You see, she lives in Cooper Springs now."

"Yeah, my father told me," Dawn said sadly.

"Your father?" I asked, with shock. "I thought he was dead."

"Mr. Thurman, my birth father," she said. "A man stopped to offer me a ride after my car broke down. I asked him to take me to Rockfish, but he said he had to make a stop first. Then he steered into the woods. That's when I started dropping candy wrappers out the window. I wasn't sure I could trust him. At first, he called me Eve. Then he told me about his wife. He said she was my birth mother. And he said that I have a twin sister."

"You do," I told her. "Eve looks just like you."

"Oh, I can't believe this is true!" she said. "Mr. Thurman seemed so nice. But then he locked me in that cabin. He said that he needed to come up with a plan. He wanted to use me to get his wife back. But he said he wasn't sure how and that he had to think. So he just left me there. That was days ago!"

"How did you manage?" I asked. "You must have been terrified."

"I screamed, but no one ever answered," she said. "There was no phone, no food. I searched and finally found an old can of soda. I tried to make it last, but I had no idea how long I'd be trapped there.

"Today, I knew I had to find my own way out. The windows were too small to crawl through, so I banged on the door. The wood was old and rotting. So after pushing and banging for hours, I felt the hinge starting to loosen. I put my back against the door and pushed as hard as I could. The crack near the hinge got a little bigger. So I wedged a piece of wood in and pushed on it till the hinge popped off.

"But by then, I was tired and thirsty. There was no way I'd make it down this trail without a drink. And well, you know the rest."

"So you haven't seen Mr. Thurman since he left?" I asked Dawn.

"No," she said. "He just took off. He must be crazy!"

Finally, we were back at the road. I filled Dawn in on our search while we walked toward my car. But before we got there, Sam and Julie drove up.

"Hey! Is that you, Dawn?" Julie hollered out the window.

The sisters were hugging as soon as the car stopped. We got in to ride the rest of the way back to my car.

Julie and Sam had already found Mr. Thurman in Rockfish. Finding his other daughter had proved too much for him. He'd been wandering around town babbling about his two daughters. Everyone assumed he was seeing things or having a breakdown. So he'd been put under a doctor's care.

When we got to my car, I asked Dawn if she was ready to go home.

"Actually," she said, "I've come a long way and been through an awful lot. It would be a shame not to see the person I've been looking for. Please take me to Mrs. Thurman's house. I'll call Mom from there and tell her I'm OK."

"Do you know that I've met your sister?" Julie asked.

"You've met my twin?" Dawn gasped.

"Yes," said Julie. "She's as beautiful as you are. You're going to love her. And now I've got two sisters!"

I decided to let them go along to Cooper Springs without me. Chance and I got out of Sam's car.

"I'll let everyone at home know you're OK, Dawn," I said. "Be sure and call your mom. She'll be awfully glad to hear your voice again."

As Sam drove away, I could hear Julie and Dawn chattering about their adventures. Luckily no one was hurt. And maybe now two small families could come together.

Chance and I got in my car. We were both wiped out. All I could think about was rocking myself to sleep in the old chair on Mamaw's porch. "Hey, Chance, what do you say we have a nap when we get home?" I asked.

But when I turned to look at Chance, he was already asleep.

Tony Jefferson